9
MAGIC WISHES

illustrated by **LORRAINE FOX**

A MODERN MASTERS BOOK FOR CHILDREN

THE CROWELL-COLLIER PRESS

SHiRLEY JACKSON

9

MAGiC WiSHES

First Crowell-Collier Press Edition 1963

Library of Congress Catalog Card Number: 63-8302
Copyright © 1963 by Shirley Jackson
Illustrations Copyright © 1963 by The Crowell-Collier
Publishing Company

Today was a very funny day.

The sky was green and the sun was blue and all the trees were flying balloons. A magician came walking down my street. His coat was long and black and there were stars on his hat.

"I will give you nine wishes," the magician

said to me. "What do you wish for?"

So I closed my eyes and wished.

Wish one was for an orange pony with a purple tail. He ran as fast as the wind and his eyes were blue.

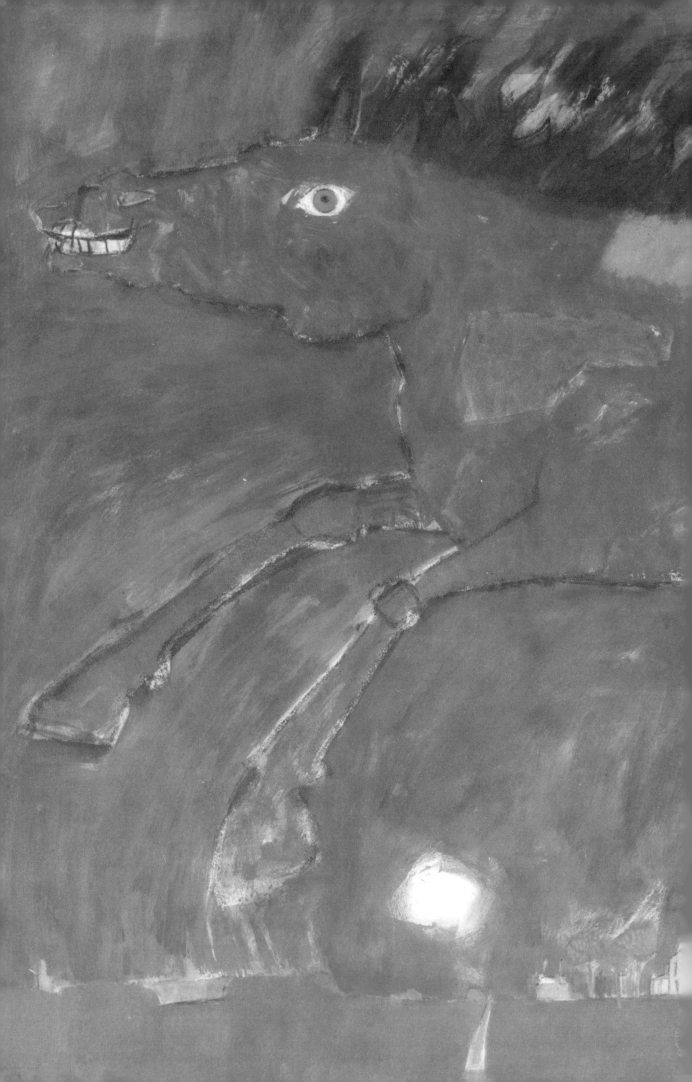

Wish two was for a squirrel holding a nut

that opens and inside is a Christmas tree.

Wish three was for a round little clown with a butterfly on his nose. The clown knew tricks and songs and games and the butterfly stayed on his nose.

Wish four was for a garden of flowers all made of candy. I ate a sugar rose and a candy cane tree.

Wish five was for a snowman with a black hat and eyes of coal. He was so cold that I put on my mittens before I shook his hand.

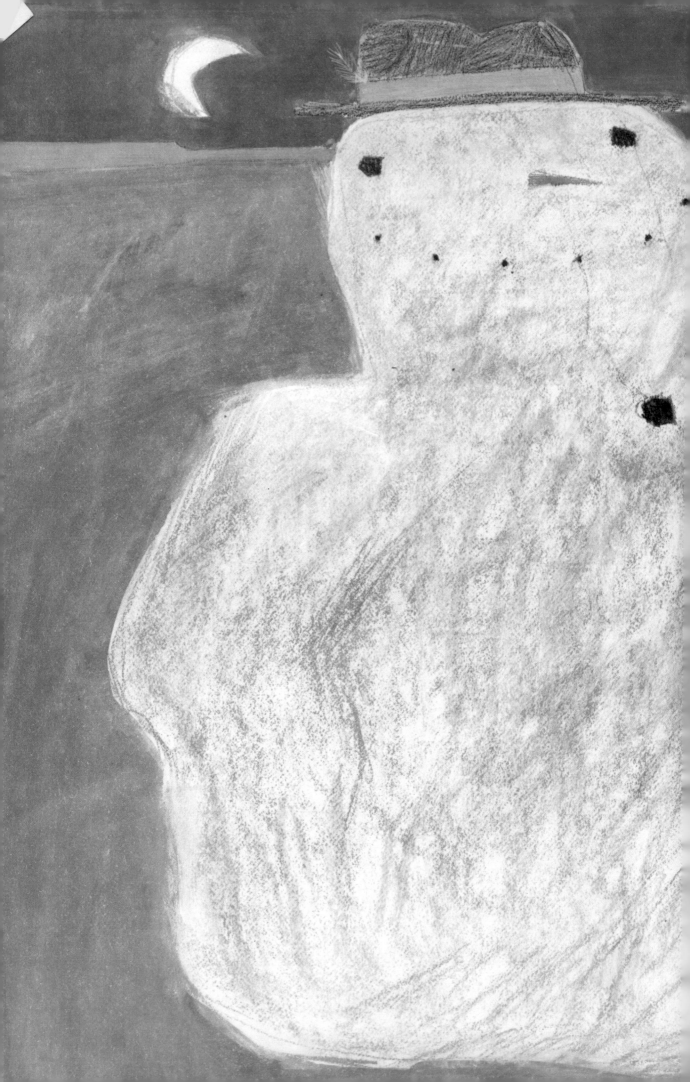

Wish six was for a tiny zoo all for me, with a tiger and a lion and a bear. They were all so small I could put them in my pocket.

Wish seven was for a silver ship with sails of red and it carried me in the air over the tops of the trees and the tops of the houses and everybody on the ground thought I was a bird.

Wish eight was for a little box and inside is
another box and inside is another box and
inside is another box and inside that is
an elephant.

"But that is only eight wishes," the magician said to me. "You may have one more wish."

But I had an orange pony with a purple tail and a squirrel holding a nut with a Christmas tree inside and a round little clown with a butterfly on his nose and a garden of flowers all made of candy and a cold cold snowman and a tiny zoo all my own and a silver ship with sails of red and a little box with another box inside and another box inside and another box inside and inside that an elephant.

"Thank you," I said to the magician, "but there is really nothing more to wish for."

"Then there is one wish left," the magician said to me. "I will put it here on this rock and somebody will find it and have a magic wish."

Then he turned himself into a leaf and the wind blew him away.

Today was a very, very funny day.

MODERN MASTERS BOOKS FOR CHILDREN

PHYLLIS McGINLEY
  The B Book (Illustrated by Robert Jones)
ROBERT GRAVES
  The Big Green Book (Illustrated by Maurice Sendak)
LOUIS UNTERMEYER
  One And One And One (Illustrated by Robert Jones)
JAY WILLIAMS
  Puppy Pie (Illustrated by Wayne Blickenstaff)
WILLIAM JAY SMITH
  What Did I See? (Illustrated by Don Almquist)
JOHN CIARDI
  The Wish-Tree (Illustrated by Lou Glanzman)
SHIRLEY JACKSON
  Nine Magic Wishes (Illustrated by Lorraine Fox)
PAUL ENGLE
  Who's Afraid? (Illustrated by Ray Prohaska)
EVE MERRIAM
  Funny Town (Illustrated by Evaline Ness)
ARTHUR MILLER
  Jane's Blanket (Illustrated by Al Parker)
WILLIAM SAROYAN
  Me (Illustrated by Murray Tinkelman)
THEODORE ROETHKE
  Party at the Zoo (Illustrated by Al Swiller)
RICHARD WILBUR
  Loudmouse (Illustrated by Don Almquist)
ISAAC ASIMOV
  The Best New Thing (Illustrated by Bruce Bomberger)
PEARL S. BUCK
  The Little Fox in the Middle (Illustrated by Robert Jones)
ERSKINE CALDWELL
  The Deer at Our House (Illustrated by Ben Wohlberg)
MARK VAN DOREN
  Somebody Came (Illustrated by Lorraine Fox)
MARY ELLEN CHASE
  Thank-you Is a Lovely Word (Illustrated by Bernard D'Andrea)